THE BIG GAME

Adapted by Annie Auerbach
Illustrated by the Disney Storybook Artists
Designed by Tony Fejeran of Disney Publishing's Global Design Group

A Random House PICTUREBACK® Book

Random House 🏠 New York

Library of Congress Control Number: 2004115058
ISBN: 0-7364-2322-2

www.randomhouse.com/kids/disney

Printed in the United States of America
10 9 8 7 6 5 4 3 2 1

It was the bottom of the ninth inning. Goosey Loosey was on third base, and the Acorns needed just one run to tie the big game.

In the dugout, Chicken Little smiled. After all the humiliation following the sky-is-falling incident, he was sure that a win would make his father, Buck, proud—even though Chicken Little hadn't played at all in the game. His dad loved baseball. In fact, Buck had been the star of the Acorns when they last defeated the Spud Valley Taters, twenty years ago!

"Up next . . . **Chicken Little**."

Chicken Little was excited. He had been sitting patiently on the bench for a long time—and he had not expected to have a chance at bat in the big game! But the coach had no choice. The rest of the players were already in the game or on the injured list.

The fans groaned. Chicken Little had a reputation for starting trouble, not hitting home runs.

"He's gonna lose the game for us!" someone complained.

Determined, Chicken Little thought of his father.

"I won't embarrass you, Dad," he whispered. "Not this time."

Then Chicken Little stepped up to the plate. The pitcher wound up and threw the ball! Chicken Little barely managed to swing the bat . . . long after the ball landed in the catcher's glove.

"**Strike one!**" called the umpire.

The crowd gasped. The Taters laughed out loud!

Next, the pitcher threw a curveball low and outside. Chicken Little swung. . . .

"**Strike two!**" called the umpire.

One more strike and the game would be over.

Chicken Little took a deep breath. He knew he had one more chance to make his dad proud.

"Today is a new day," he told himself as the pitcher wound up.

He gathered his strength and swung with all his might. **Crack!** A hit!

"Run, kid, run!" the announcer shouted.

"Go, go, go!" the crowd chanted.

Then Chicken Little heard his father, Buck, calling from the stands. "Go, son! **Run! Run!**"

Chicken Little started running . . . but in the wrong direction!

"No, no! Not that way! Run the other way!" yelled Buck.

Chicken Little turned and ran toward first base.
Goosey Loosey took off from third base and
raced to home plate.
"We have a tie game!" cried the announcer.
Chicken Little kept going. He was a chicken on
a mission!
"Today's a **new** day!" he chanted to himself.

"**Mayhem** in the outfield, ladies and gentlemen," the announcer said as the Spud Valley Taters scrambled for the ball. When they finally found it—stuck on the center fielder's horn—they tipped over the bull and started running toward Chicken Little. It was going to be a close call!

Whoosh! Chicken Little slid toward home plate.

Thunk! The bull landed on home plate.

Whomp! A huge pile of dirt covered Chicken Little as the bull tagged him with the ball.

Chicken Little was **out!**

Or was he? The umpire yelled, "**Wait!**"

The crowd hushed as the umpire started brushing the dirt off Chicken Little and home plate.

"**Safe!**" the umpire called. "The runner is safe!"

"There's a new winner in town, and his name is Chicken Little!" the announcer shouted.

"Yes, yes, yes!" Buck said proudly as the crowd cheered. "That's my boy!"

At last, the town's littlest chicken had become its **biggest hero!**